My Pony Book

Dawn McMillan

Contents

Ponies

This is my pony.
His name is Flash.

I like ponies.
Ponies are good pets.

A pony is a little horse.

horse

pony

I can name the parts of a pony.

ears

mane

face

tail

hoof

Looking after Ponies

I like to look after Flash.

I brush Flash with a brush.

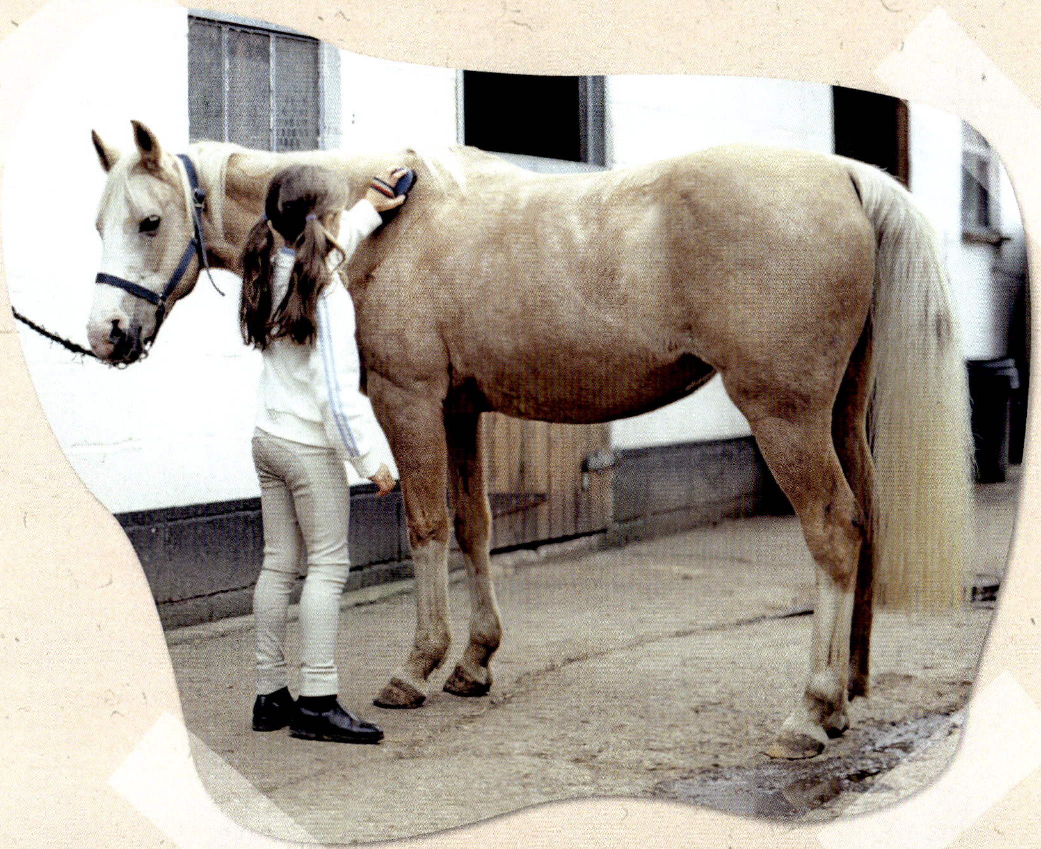

I brush Flash's coat.

I get the stones from Flash's feet.
A pony's foot is called a hoof.

I use this pick to clean Flash's hoof.

A pony needs a place to live.
Flash lives in a field.

A pony needs food to eat.
I give Flash some food.

hay

water

I give Flash some water, too.

Riding Ponies

I like to ride Flash.

We go round the ring.

I ride Flash and play games.

Flash did well in the games.
We got a ribbon!

Things to Do for Flash

- Brush Flash and clean his feet.
- Ride Flash.
- Give Flash food and water.
- Give Flash a hug!